SPORTS SUPERSTARS
JOE BURROW

BY THOMAS K. ADAMSON

BELLWETHER MEDIA·MINNEAPOLIS, MN

Torque brims with excitement perfect for thrill-seekers of all kinds. Discover daring survival skills, explore uncharted worlds, and marvel at mighty engines and extreme sports. In *Torque* books, anything can happen. Are you ready?

This edition first published in 2023 by Bellwether Media, Inc.

No part of this publication may be reproduced in whole or in part without written permission of the publisher. For information regarding permission, write to Bellwether Media, Inc., Attention: Permissions Department, 6012 Blue Circle Drive, Minnetonka, MN 55343.

Library of Congress Cataloging-in-Publication Data

Names: Adamson, Thomas K., 1970- author.
Title: Joe Burrow / by Thomas K. Adamson.
Description: Minneapolis, MN : Bellwether Media, 2023. | Series: Torque. Sports superstars | Includes bibliographical references and index. | Audience: Ages 7-12 | Audience: Grades 4-6 | Summary: "Engaging images accompany information about Joe Burrow. The combination of high-interest subject matter and light text is intended for students in grades 3 through 7"– Provided by publisher.
Identifiers: LCCN 2022050063 (print) | LCCN 2022050064 (ebook) | ISBN 9798886871555 (library binding) | ISBN 9798886872811 (ebook)
Subjects: LCSH: Burrow, Joe, 1996–Juvenile literature. | Quarterbacks (Football)–United States–Biography–Juvenile literature.
Classification: LCC GV939.B873 A73 2023 (print) | LCC GV939.B873 (ebook) | DDC 796.332092 [B]–dc23/eng/20221019
LC record available at https://lccn.loc.gov/2022050063
LC ebook record available at https://lccn.loc.gov/2022050064

Text copyright © 2023 by Bellwether Media, Inc. TORQUE and associated logos are trademarks and/or registered trademarks of Bellwether Media, Inc.

Editor: Kieran Downs   Designer: Josh Brink

Printed in the United States of America, North Mankato, MN.

TABLE OF CONTENTS

A JOE COOL COMEBACK	4
WHO IS JOE BURROW?	6
EARLY SPORTS SUCCESS	8
A YOUNG STAR	12
A BRIGHT FUTURE	20
GLOSSARY	22
TO LEARN MORE	23
INDEX	24

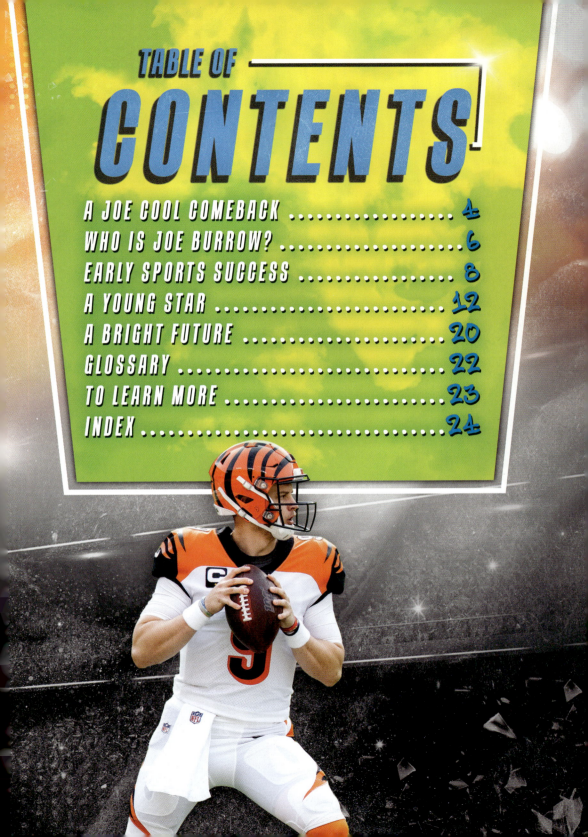

A JOE COOL COMEBACK

Joe Burrow stays calm. It is the 2022 **conference championship game**. The Cincinnati Bengals trail the Kansas City Chiefs. He throws the ball. Ja'Marr Chase leaps and catches it for a **touchdown**! Burrow then ties the game with a two-point pass to Trent Taylor.

The Bengals go on to win the game. They are going to the **Super Bowl**!

Super Comeback

The Bengals trailed the Chiefs 21–3 at one point in the first half of the game.

WHO IS JOE BURROW?

Joe Burrow is a **quarterback** in the **National Football League** (NFL). In only his second season, he led the Cincinnati Bengals to Super Bowl 56. Burrow is known for being calm under **pressure**. It earned him the nickname "Joe Cool."

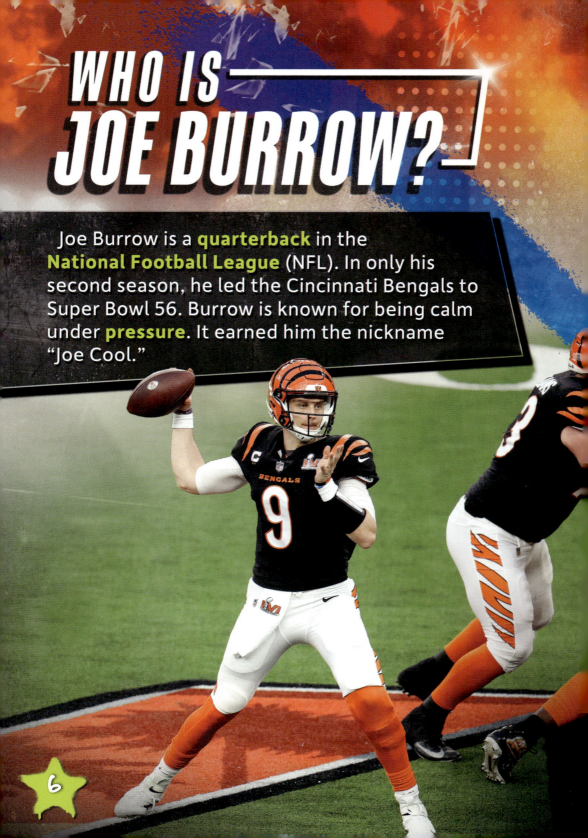

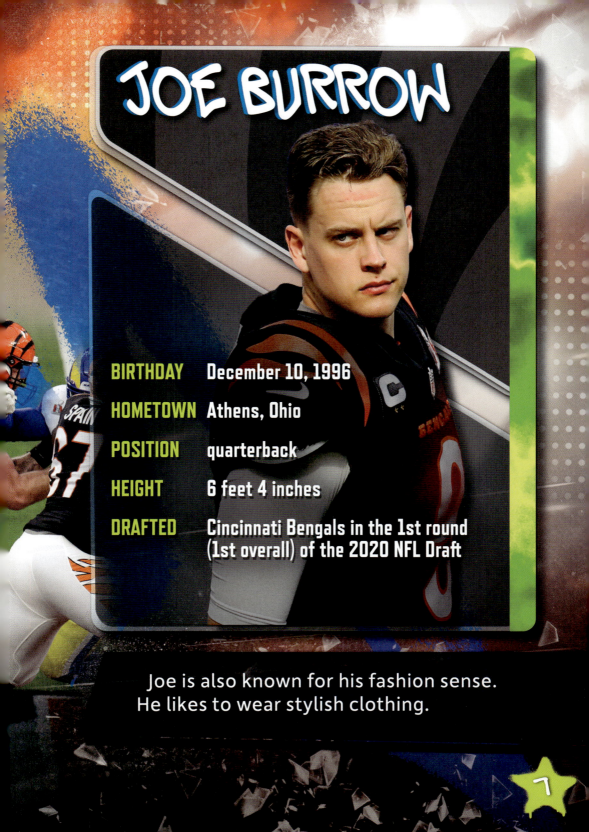

EARLY SPORTS SUCCESS

Burrow always loved sports. In third grade, he wanted to play other positions in football. He thought he would get the ball more. But his coach made him play quarterback.

All-Around Athlete
Burrow also played basketball in high school. As a senior, he averaged 19.3 points per game.

Burrow continued playing quarterback through high school. He led his team to the **playoffs** three straight years.

Burrow started playing college football at Ohio State. He did not win the starting position. He moved to Louisiana State University (LSU).

In his senior year at LSU, Burrow threw for 5,671 yards. He threw 60 touchdown passes and only 6 **interceptions**. He led LSU to a national championship. Burrow also won the **Heisman Trophy**.

Joe's Great Game

In 2019, Burrow threw 7 touchdown passes in one game. He also ran for another touchdown in that game.

PET	FOOD	BOARD GAME	CARTOON

miniature goldendoodle	anything spicy	chess	SpongeBob SquarePants

HEISMAN TROPHY

A YOUNG STAR

Burrow was picked first overall in the 2020 NFL **Draft**. The Bengals made Burrow their starting quarterback. He was on pace to break many NFL **rookie** records.

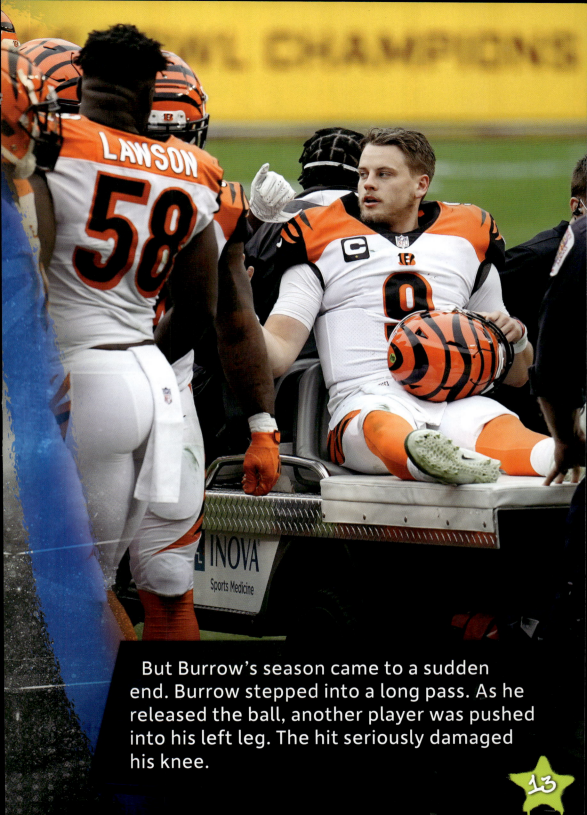

But Burrow's season came to a sudden end. Burrow stepped into a long pass. As he released the ball, another player was pushed into his left leg. The hit seriously damaged his knee.

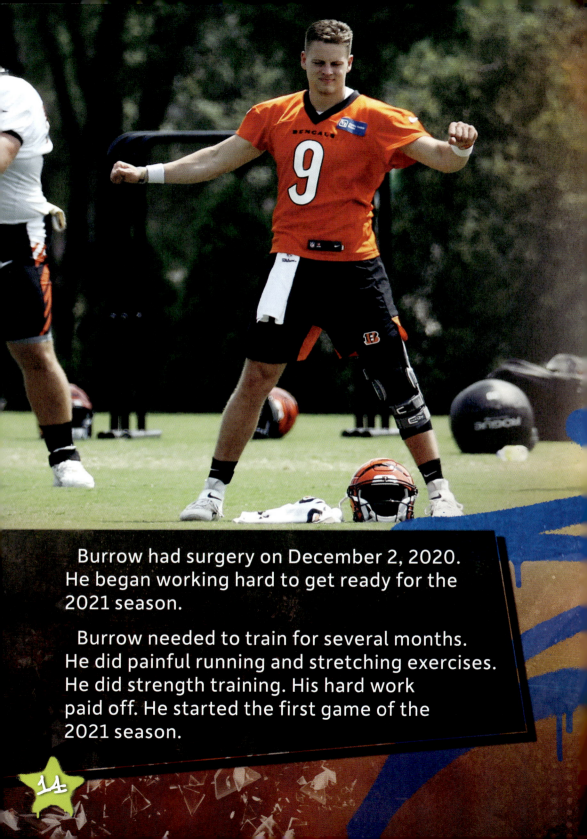

Burrow had surgery on December 2, 2020. He began working hard to get ready for the 2021 season.

Burrow needed to train for several months. He did painful running and stretching exercises. He did strength training. His hard work paid off. He started the first game of the 2021 season.

Burrow came back strong in 2021. He had the highest pass completion **percentage** in the NFL. He also threw for 4,611 yards.

Burrow led the Bengals to 10 wins. This gave the team a spot in the playoffs. His play earned him the Comeback Player of the Year award.

Burrow led the Bengals to their first playoff win since 1990. The team continued to play well. They beat the Kansas City Chiefs in the conference championship game. This got them to the Super Bowl!

Unfortunately, the Bengals ran into a tough Rams team. They narrowly lost after a late touchdown by the Rams.

Pre-Game Routines

Burrow eats a caramel apple sucker before each game. He also wears one sock inside-out.

TIMELINE

December 2019
Burrow wins the Heisman Trophy

January 2020
Burrow wins the college national championship

September 2020
Burrow plays his first NFL game

November 2020

Burrow injures his knee

January 2022

The Bengals win the AFC Conference Championship Game

February 2022

The Bengals lose to the Rams in Super Bowl 56

A BRIGHT FUTURE

Burrow loves having the responsibility of being a team leader. He showed his toughness in coming back from a terrible knee injury. He helped make the Bengals a feared team in the NFL again.

Burrow is hopeful for the Bengals' future. He believes the Bengals will be back in the Super Bowl!

GLOSSARY

conference championship game—a game that decides which team will play in the Super Bowl

draft—a process during which professional teams choose high school and college athletes to play for them

Heisman Trophy—an award that goes to the best college football player of the season

interceptions—passes thrown by the offensive team that are caught by the defensive team

National Football League—a professional football league in the United States; the National Football League is often called the NFL.

percentage—a part of something, expressed as a number out of one hundred

playoffs—games played after the regular season is over; playoff games determine which teams play in the championship game.

pressure—stress or urgency

quarterback—a player on offense whose main job is to throw and hand off the ball

rookie—a first year player in a sports league

Super Bowl—the annual championship game of the National Football League

touchdown—a score that occurs when a team crosses into their opponent's end zone with the football; a touchdown is worth six points.

TO LEARN MORE

AT THE LIBRARY

Bailey, Diane. *The Story of the Cincinnati Bengals.* Minneapolis, Minn.: Kaleidoscope, 2020.

Coleman, Ted. *Cincinnati Bengals All-Time Greats.* Mendota Heights, Minn.: North Star Editions, 2022.

Fishman, Jon M. *Joe Burrow.* Minneapolis, Minn.: Lerner Publications, 2022.

ON THE WEB

FACTSURFER

Factsurfer.com gives you a safe, fun way to find more information.

1. Go to www.factsurfer.com

2. Enter "Joe Burrow" into the search box and click 🔍.

3. Select your book cover to see a list of related content.

INDEX

awards, 10, 11, 16, 17
basketball, 8
childhood, 8, 9
Cincinnati Bengals, 4, 5, 6, 12, 16, 18, 20, 21
conference championship game, 4, 5, 18
draft, 12
favorites, 11
future, 21
Heisman Trophy, 10, 11
injury, 13, 20
Louisiana State University, 10
map, 15
National Football League, 6, 12, 16, 20
nickname, 6

Ohio State, 10
playoffs, 9, 16, 18
profile, 7
quarterback, 6, 8, 9, 12
records, 12
rookie, 12
routines, 18
Super Bowl, 4, 6, 18, 21
surgery, 14
timeline, 18–19
touchdown, 4, 10, 18
trophy shelf, 17

The images in this book are reproduced through the courtesy of: Cal Sport Media/ Alamy, front cover(hero), p. 10; AlexanderJonesi/ Wiki Commons, p. 3; David Eulitt/ Stringer/ Getty Images, p. 4; Icon Sportswire/ Contributor/ Getty Images, p. 5; Michael Owens/ Getty Images, p. 6; Kevin C. Cox/ Staff/ Getty Images, pp. 7 (Burrow), 20; Cincinnati Bengals/ Wiki Commons, p. 7 (Bengals stripes); Juan Lainez/ Marinmedia/ Csm/ AP Images, p. 8; Scott W. Grau/ Icon Sportswire/ AP Images, p. 9; SoySendra, p. 11 (pet); Silvy78, p. 11 (food); Will Thomass, p. 11 (board game); Evelina Shu, p. 11 (cartoon); lev radin, p. 11; UPI/ Alamy, pp. 12, 18 (January 2020); Patrick McDermott/ Getty Images, p. 13; Dylan Buell/ Stringer/ Getty Images, p. 14; Harold Stiver, p. 15 (Cincinnati, Ohio); Dylan Buell/ Contributor/ Getty Images, p. 15; Andy Lyons/ Staff/ Getty Images, pp. 16, 18-19, 21; Jamie Squire/ Staff/ Getty Images, p. 17; The White House/ Wiki Commons, p. 18 (December 2019); Mitchell Leff/ Stringer/ Getty Images, p. 19 (November 2020); Au Kirk/ Wiki Commons, p. 19 (January 2022); Wawx, p. 19 (February 2022); All-Pro Reels/ Wiki Commons, p. 23.

24